The Easter Bunny Gang

Story & Illustrations by
Jane & Dale Baer
The Baer Animation Company

For the Children
of
The Stony Mountain
Elementary
School

Ideals Publishing Corp.
Milwaukee, Wisconsin

Copyright © MCMLXXXIII The Baer Animation Company
All rights reserved. Printed and bound in U.S.A.
Published simultaneously in Canada.
ISBN 0-8249-8048-4

The first day of Easter Egg Painting Season had arrived. Easter was just a few weeks away. The bunnies had worked hard for months gathering and hauling eggs to the storage vaults beneath the old cottonwood tree.

It was a lovely spring morning to hold a painting party. But the party was not to be ... for that was the year of the BIG BURGLARY!

The members of the Easter Bunny Gang awoke early that morning. They raced to the cottonwood tree, eager to see how the new egg-dipping computer worked. They could hardly wait to begin decorating the eggs that would roll out, all dyed with bright colors.

When they reached the tree, Violet noticed that something was wrong. "Oh, my!" she gasped. "Someone has left the door wide open!"

Willie, Rigby, Rosemary, and Barnaby Bunny cautiously peered through the doorway.

Slowly the bunnies made their way down the dark, winding passageway that led to the egg vaults. Every door along the tunnel had been left open, but nothing was out of place. The great mountains of eggs were neatly stacked just as the bunnies had left them.

Further along the tunnel, they stepped inside the painting room. Everything seemed to be in order. The computer was all set to go. Aprons were hanging from their hooks. The egg designs were pinned to the walls. But... something was missing.

Suddenly the bunnies knew what it was. "OUR PAINT IS GONE!" they cried out. "SOMEONE HAS STOLEN OUR PAINT!"

Rosemary sounded the alarm.

Rigby discovered the first clue. "Hmmm," he said, thoughtfully. "It looks like the thieves dropped this paint can while they were making their getaway."

He picked up a magnifying glass and examined the puddle closely. The bunnies crowded around. Peering through the glass, they saw footprints that led across the room and out the doorway.

"I have a theory about this," said Rigby.

$\mathcal{A}$t that moment, the thumpity-thumping sounds of many rabbits' feet echoed throughout the passageway as the older bunnies hurried to the scene of the burglary.

"What's going on here?" demanded Mr. Wuzzelfuzz, the first to arrive. "Who sounded the alarm?"

The other bunnies crowded into the room just in time to hear Violet say "stolen paint." A great hullabaloo broke out, drowning out the rest of her story.

"Thieves?"

"Who could have done such a thing?"

"We can't deliver plain white eggs to the children!"

"Easter will be ruined!"

None of the older bunnies noticed the strange footprints or bothered listening to Rigby's theory about them. The young bunnies hopped out into the passageway.

"Let's follow the villains while their trail is red-hot," said Rigby. "These footprints should lead us directly to our missing paint and the missing paint thieves."

The bunnies all agreed.

"Come on, gang," said Rosemary. "Let's follow Rigby."

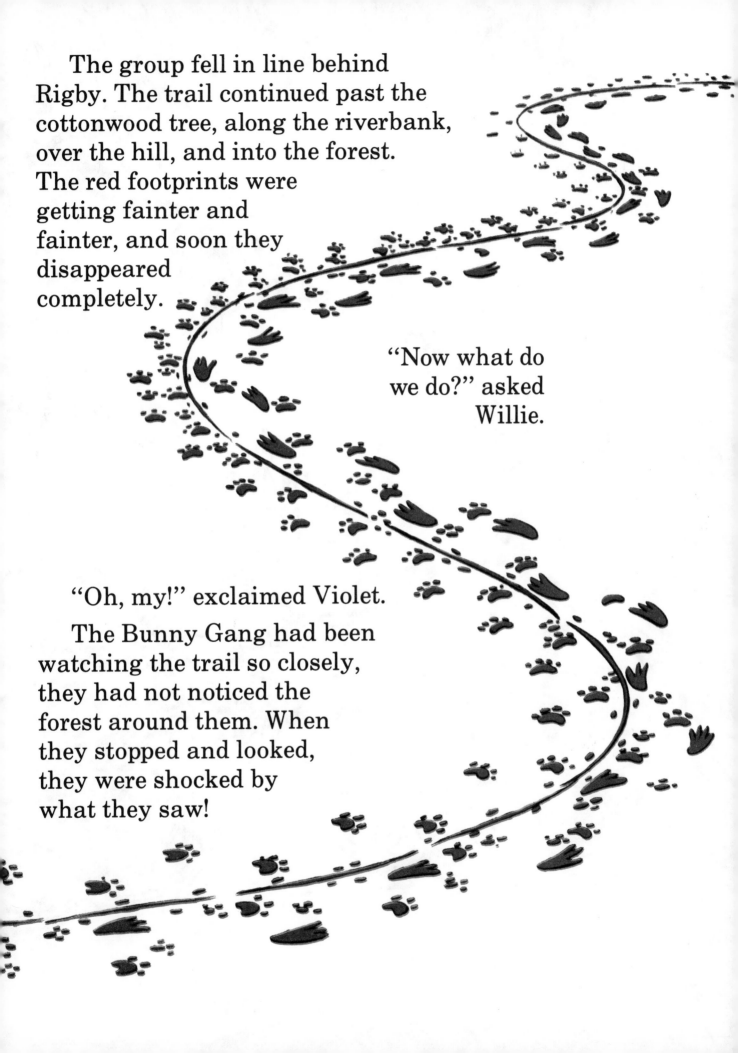

The group fell in line behind Rigby. The trail continued past the cottonwood tree, along the riverbank, over the hill, and into the forest. The red footprints were getting fainter and fainter, and soon they disappeared completely.

"Now what do we do?" asked Willie.

"Oh, my!" exclaimed Violet.

The Bunny Gang had been watching the trail so closely, they had not noticed the forest around them. When they stopped and looked, they were shocked by what they saw!

Everything in the forest was covered with scribbling!

"How could anybody do such a thing?" said Violet. "They even used our paint!"

"What do they mean, they don't like Easter eggs?" said Rosemary. "Everyone likes Easter eggs."

"Why don't they like us bunnies?" asked Barnaby.

"We must stop these vandals before they destroy any more of the forest!" said Rigby.

The Bunny Gang raced back to the cottonwood tree as fast as they could hop. They were amazed to find the older rabbits still in the same place, all talking at once and worrying about what would happen on Easter morning. But ... no one was talking about a way to solve the problem.

The young bunnies knew it was impossible to get their attention. They hopped down the tunnel to the cellar in search of a quiet place to think. They gathered around a dusty, wobbly old table. Rigby began to speak.

"We must think of a plan to stop the destruction of our forest!" cried Rigby. "We must remove the ugly graffiti, and, most of all, we must find our paint before it is all used up!" To make his point, Rigby pounded the tabletop with his paw, sending up a dusty cloud that started everybody sneezing.

When the bunnies settled down, Rigby asked for suggestions. They all thought and thought and thought, but not one of them could think of a plan.

Tired from the morning's excitement, Barnaby leaned back to rest against the old egg-dipping machine. It had been replaced by the new computer and stored in the cellar. His paw accidentally hit the starter switch.

With a pop and a sputter and a bang, the dipping arms cranked into motion. Soon the old tub was chugging at such a furious speed that it began dancing around the cellar.

Barnaby was so startled, he shot up into the air and banged his head on a ceiling beam.

"That's the answer!" shouted Rigby. "What a wonderful idea! Barnaby, you've saved the day!"

"It is? What is? I have?" asked Barnaby, looking terribly confused.

"Don't you see?" said Rigby, hopping up and down and pointing to the dancing machine. "All we need to do is make a few adjustments and an addition here and there."

The Bunny Gang set to work immediately.

First, they drew up their plan, and then ...

... they cleaned off the workbench and brought out the tools. They had no time to lose!

The bunnies worked late into the night. Just before sunrise, they threw open the door of the cottonwood tree and dragged out a large, mysterious-looking contraption. Slowly they made their way along the riverbank. They pulled it over the hill into the unsightly forest, covered with ugly drawings and scribblings. The bunnies trudged on, trying not to look at the shameful sight.

Finally they came upon a beautiful place deep in the forest. It was just what they had been searching for. There was no trace of graffiti there.

The Bunny Gang had no
time to waste. They quickly
hung some signs they
had made. The bunnies
pushed their contraption
out of sight behind the
bushes, and then they
hid and waited.

$\mathcal{B}$efore long, they heard a loud commotion. A group of scruffy animals appeared on the pathway carrying buckets of paint and brushes and spray cans. When they saw the signs, they stopped.

"Where did these signs come from? Who says we can't paint here?" the bunnies heard them muttering. Then the vandals dipped their paintbrushes into the buckets, opened the spray cans, and began to paint over the signs.

"I bet those bunnies had something to do with this. We'll show them! Nobody can tell us what to do!" said one of the troublemakers, kicking over a sign. "We can paint wherever we want."

Just as he was about to spray a tree with a can of purple paint, the Bunny Gang pulled the covering away from their contraption, flipped the starter switch, and …

... a giant robot whirred into action! Huge, mechanical arms reached over and around the bushes, lifting the startled vandals off their feet and swinging them into the air. Mechanical fingers snatched up the paint and brushes. Before they knew what was happening, the paint thieves found themselves dipped, brushed, and sprayed as brightly as an assortment of Easter eggs.

"Let me go! Help! Put me down!" yelled the captives, but the robot held them high above the ground.

The bunnies sprang out from their hiding place. "You won't be released until you tell us where you've hidden the rest of our Easter egg paint!" said Rigby.

"Okay, okay, we'll tell you. Don't hurt us!" begged the frightened animals, squirming uncomfortably.

"You must also promise to scrub off all the graffiti and clean up the forest," said Rigby.

That afternoon a most unusual parade marched up to the old cottonwood tree. The older rabbits rushed to greet the young heroes. For the first time, they were willing to listen to the Bunny Gang. The young bunnies told them all about their adventures.

When the paint was safely brought back to the painting room, the bunnies turned to their captives. Mr. Wuzzelfuzz paced back and forth in front of the group. He looked at them sternly over the top of his glasses.

"What made you do such a dreadful thing?" he asked. "You almost spoiled Easter for all the boys and girls!"

The troublemakers hung their heads with shame.

"Maybe Easter would be spoiled for some of the boys and girls," said Molly Mink in a small voice, "but we never get Easter eggs anyway."

"Stuff and nonsense and fiddledeedee!" Mr. Wuzzelfuzz blustered. "That's pure poppycock! All boys and girls get Easter eggs on Easter morning."

"Everyone, except us forest critters. We're kids too," said Spike Porcupine, wiping away a tear.

"Why, this is terrible," sputtered Mr. Wuzzelfuzz. "Of course, there are children in the forest, too. How could we be so thoughtless?"

Rigby quickly spoke up. "I think we owe these kids an apology," he said, turning to the forlorn animals. "I have an idea. If you will help us decorate our Easter eggs, we will help you clean up the forest."

Everyone thought that was a wonderful idea, and the egg-painting party finally began.